I0741565

Goldie,
Max & Milk

by Karen Hartman

FOR PRODUCTION INQUIRIES

UNITED STATES AND CANADA
info@concordtheatricals.com
1-866-979-0447

UNITED KINGDOM AND EUROPE
licensing@concordtheatricals.co.uk
020-7054-7298

Each title is subject to availability from Concord Theatricals Corp., depending upon country of performance. Please be aware that *GOLDIE, MAX & MILK* may not be licensed by Concord Theatricals Corp. in your territory. Professional and amateur producers should contact the nearest Concord Theatricals Corp. office or licensing partner to verify availability.

No one shall make any changes in this title(s) for the purpose of production. No part of this book may be reproduced, stored in a retrieval system, scanned, uploaded, or transmitted in any form, by any means, now known or yet to be invented, including mechanical, electronic, digital, photocopying, recording, videotaping, or otherwise, without the prior written permission of the publisher. No one shall share this title(s), or any part of this title(s), through any social media or file hosting websites.

For all inquiries regarding motion picture, television, online/digital and other media rights, please contact Concord Theatricals Corp.

MUSIC AND THIRD-PARTY MATERIALS USE NOTE

Licensees are solely responsible for obtaining formal written permission from copyright owners to use copyrighted music and/or other copyrighted third-party materials (e.g. artworks, logos) in the performance of this play and are strongly cautioned to do so. If no such permission is obtained by the licensee, then the licensee must use only original music and materials that the licensee owns and controls. Licensees are solely responsible and liable for clearances of all third-party copyrighted materials, including without limitation music, and shall indemnify the copyright owners of the play(s) and their licensing agent, Concord Theatricals Corp., against any costs, expenses, losses and liabilities arising from the use of such copyrighted third-party materials by licensees. For music, please contact the appropriate music licensing authority in your territory for the rights to any incidental music.

IMPORTANT BILLING AND CREDIT REQUIREMENTS

If you have obtained performance rights to this title, please refer to your licensing agreement for important billing and credit requirements.

GOLDIE, MAX & MILK premiered at Florida Stage Company (Louis Tyrrell, Producing Director; Nancy Barnett, Managing Director) and The Phoenix Theatre (Bryan Fonseca, Producing Director; Sharon Gamble, Managing Director), and was selected for a National New Play Network Rolling World Premiere.

The Florida Stage production opened at the Kravis Center for the Performing Arts in West Palm Beach, Florida, on December 15, 2010. The production was directed by Margaret Ledford, with scenic design by Timothy R. Mackabee, lighting design by Jim Hunter, sound design by Matt Kelly, and costume design by Michiko Skinner. The stage manager was James Danford. The cast was as follows:

MAX	Erin Joy Schmidt
GOLDIE	Deborah Sherman
MIKE	David Hemphill
LISA	Carla Harting
SHAYNA	Sarah Lord

The Phoenix Theatre production opened in Indianapolis, Indiana, on February 3, 2011. The production was directed by Bryan Fonseca, with set design by Dan Tracy, lighting design by Laura Glover, sound design by Tim Brickley and Matt Kelly, and costume design by Ashley Kiefer. The stage manager was Anthony Morton. The cast was as follows:

MAX	Sara Riemen
GOLDIE	Wendy Farber
MIKE	Kienan McCartney
LISA	Angela Plank
SHAYNA	Bridgette Richards

The Off Broadway premiere of *GOLDIE, MAX & MILK* was produced by Mary J. Davis and MBL Productions, and opened at 59E59 Theaters on May 1, 2022. The play was presented as part of 59E59 Theaters' first annual AMPLIFY Festival (formerly VOLT) celebrating the work of Karen Hartman. The production was directed by Jackson Gay, with scenic design by Junghyun Georgia Lee, costume design by Junghyun Georgia Lee & Ilana Breitman, lighting design by Kate McGee, sound design by Sun Hee Kil, and props design by Nick Campano. Casting was by Stephanie Klapper Casting, the general manager was Dailey-Monda Management, the production stage manager was Caroline Ragland, the assistant stage manager was Julie Gottfried, and the assistant director was Alexander Coddington. The cast was as follows:

MAX. . . . . Shayna Small
GOLDIE. . . . . Lauren Molina
MIKE . . . . .Timiki Salinas
LISA . . . . Blair Baker
SHAYNA . . . . Beatrice Ethel Tulchin
Understudy for **MAX, GOLDIE, LISA, SHAYNA** . .Victoria Huston-Elem
Understudy for **MIKE** . . . . Nick Piacente

GOLDIE, MAX & MILK was developed with support from New Dramatists and the Playwrights' Center.

GOLDIE, MAX & MILK was nominated for the American Theatre Critics/Steinberg New Play Award for best regional play in America, and a Carbonell Award for the best new play in Florida.

ACKNOWLEDGMENTS

The author wishes to thank:

Val Day for envisioning the AMPLIFY Festival.

Elissa Gootman; Freda Rosenfeld; Paul Rosenfield; my siblings Aaron, Ben, and Katie Hartman; and my New York City writer's group.

For getting this book into your hands: Skyler Gray, plus the team at Samuel French/Concord Theatricals especially Amy Rose Marsh, Garrett Anderson, and Ben Keiper.

CHARACTERS

MAX – Female, 30s. Big-hearted. A social worker. Postpartum, thus subject to emotional swings that are not part of her base personality.

GOLDIE – 40ish. A lactation consultant. Domineering in a comforting way. Orthodox Jewish.

MIKE – 20s. A well-meaning slacker waking up to consequences.

LISA – 30s. Max's ex and Mike's sister. A lawyer. Often seems calm, reasonable, and warm.

SHAYNA – Late teens. Goldie's daughter. Sullen but quick. (Her middle name "Brucha" is pronounced *BRUH*-khuh)

Ethnicity is open for Max, Mike, and Lisa (even though Mike and Lisa are siblings).

SETTING

Most of the action occurs in Max and Lisa's wreck of a pre-war townhouse in Brooklyn. Keep in mind that Max and Lisa are not *poor*; they are *moving* and in a mess. Some items are high-end. A glimpse of the "bones" of the house (molding, a staircase, etc) would be welcome.

Max's apartment is probably the most realistic setting; the rest can be brushstrokes.

TIME

2009.

Fun facts about 2009: 1) It's a recession and property values are down. 2) Weed use is a crime. 3) Same sex unions are not recognized in New York.

AUTHOR'S NOTES

Max is in love with her baby, so her misery in Act One never gets too dark. To quote the wise director Allison Narver, "It's not a tragedy, it's a shitshow."

Overlapping dialogue is indicated by a slash (/) where the second line begins.

for Grisha and for Todd

ACT ONE

Scene One

*(**MAX** sits rocking her newborn in a sling. **MAX**, haphazard chic under the best of circumstances, looks bad. Her home looks worse. The bottom unit of a once-elegant two-family house, it's a mess of uneven flooring, with a huge rip in the ceiling. Not a tenement, just a wreck.)*

(Perhaps a few bright baby things, like a play gym on the floor.)

*(**MAX** doesn't move so well. She sings to her baby.)*

MAX.
HUSH LITTLE BABY DON'T SAY A WORD,
MAMA'S GONNA BUY YOU SOMETHING ABSURD.
AND IF ABSURD DON'T MAKE YOU LAUGH,
MAMA'S GONNA SLICE HER FOOT IN HALF.
AND IF HER BLOODY FOOT WON'T WALK,
MAMA'S GONNA TEACH YOU HOW TO TALK.
AND IF YOUR MOUTH CAN'T MAKE THE WORDS,
MAMA'S GONNA... MAMA'S GONNA...

*(Doorbell rings. **MAX** can't quite stand up. Doorbell rings again. **MAX** rises clutching her abdomen, which is covered by a medical support belt.)*

1

(She partway unlocks the door, revealing **MIKE***, about ten years younger than* **MAX***.)*

MIKE. Hey, uh, sorry.

MAX. For what part.

MIKE. Sorry I know you're busy, uh –

MAX. I have no plans, Mike. No foreseeable plans.

MIKE. I brought some stuff?

MAX. Stuff.

MIKE. For the little one.

(Baby cries.)

He's got pipes.

MAX. That she does.

MIKE. She. Wow. Could I come in?

MAX. You have a key.

MIKE. I wouldn't use my key.

MAX. Of course not.

MIKE. I wouldn't do that.

*(***MAX***, still holding the baby, opens the door.* **MIKE** *tumbles in with large boxes.)*

MAX. Whoa.

MIKE. I came to the hospital.

MAX. I know, Mike, I just –

MIKE. I wanted to see.

MAX. It was rough for a while. A little touch and go.

MIKE. In what way touch and go? In what way *go*?

MAX. Complications. Obstructions. The cord was wrapped and the heartbeat went down.

MIKE. The *heart*beat?

MAX. Hospital caught it. Total backup. That's why I didn't do a home birth.

MIKE. You didn't do a home birth because look at your home.

MAX. That too.

MIKE. Holes in the ceiling, god knows what layers of chipped paint, untested water out of ancient pipes...

MAX. We're selling.

MIKE. In this market?

MAX. New York is strong.

MIKE. This is Brooklyn.

MAX. Everyone wants to live in Brooklyn.

MIKE. No, they don't.

MAX. Everyone with kids. Wants a house in Brooklyn.

MIKE. No one with kids wants a shithole.

     (Baby cries.)

MAX. I gotta nurse.

MIKE. I'll wait.

MAX. You have no role here, Mike.

MIKE. Can I see her?

     *(**MAX** tilts the sling so **MIKE** can see.)*

  Oh god.

MAX. Right?

     (They smile. They soften.)

MIKE. Nice work.

MAX. Nice work.

>*(They shake hands. The baby keeps crying.)*

MIKE. Oh god. You go, girl. Sing out.

>*(**MAX** begins to nurse. **MIKE** turns away and goes through shopping bags.)*

I brought gifts.

MAX. You're dealing again?

MIKE. Why would you assume –

MAX. You have no skills. You can barely use the internet. Look at your hair; you didn't suddenly get a job.

MIKE. Just weed. Very classy, secure situation I lucked into. I won't have to rent a place and host, you know, dubious clientele; this is doorman buildings. I'm basically a very welcome UPS guy. And the financing is superior cause it's a vertical operation. I'm sourcing, and delivering.

MAX. Mike –

MIKE. I got responsibilities now.

MAX. You do *not* have responsibilities.

MIKE. Did you get a carseat?

MAX. You can't leave the hospital without a carseat.

MIKE. But do you own one? Or did you borrow it?

MAX. I don't have a car anymore.

MIKE. There are trips. There are pediatric appointments and emergencies. Okay:

>*(**MIKE** pulls a carseat out of a large bag from a superstore.)*

Consumer Reports ran a study comparing all the carseats of 2009, and what they discovered is, at a crash of over thirty-five miles per hour every one of them will spit your baby onto the pavement, except for two. One of those is made in Germany and on backorder. The other one is this. The Snugride.

And what's great about the Snugride is it's part of a travel system. Meaning you have different kinds of mobility. You can lift from the handle, like so. You can set it in the stroller, like the picture. You can take a long ride.

MAX. *(The sling.)* No stroller. I'm keeping her close.

MIKE. You have to lose contact at some point, right?

(**MAX** *keeps nursing the baby.*)

This is awkward.

MAX. *(Zen as possible.)* I am holding a human being in my arm, feeding a human being from my body. "Awkward" is a town I left behind.

MIKE. Like Portland?

MAX. I guess.

MIKE. Is she supposed to still be crying?

MAX. No.

MIKE. What's up?

MAX. I don't have milk.

MIKE. Is that bad?

MAX. The hospital recommended a consultant. Goldie.

MIKE. Goldie.

MAX. I have to wait cause she doesn't work Saturdays.

MIKE. Goldie doesn't work Saturdays?

MAX. She's an Orthodox Jew.

MIKE. Whoa. I guess they'd know.

MAX. They know fuck all. My baby's starving and she doesn't work Saturdays. Jews are supposed to prize life above law.

MIKE. If you don't have milk...what are you doing?

MAX. She will bring the milk by suckling.

MIKE. Isn't that a lot of responsibility?

MAX. It's awful.

> (**MAX** *stops nursing.*)

I'm supposed to be providing her with everything, with nourishment; until four days ago she didn't even have to cry, she didn't have to breathe, or shit, or eat, she just *was* – and I just was – doing and giving everything she needed and there was like no possible way to fuck it up except by taking drugs which is so easy to avoid. I was the perfect mother. I was the perfect world. And now it's like self service. You want milk you gotta suck on nothing, make the milk come. It's cruel. It's such a cruel cruel start to this miserable life!

> (**MAX**, *who had a c-section four days ago and has barely slept, begins to lose it. Tragic for* **MAX** *but lighter for us.*)

MIKE. I'm sorry.

MAX. Don't feel sorry for ME. Feel sorry for HER!

MIKE. Okay...

MAX. SHE's the one beginning life in a toxic unfixed fixer-upper! SHE's the one with an unemployed lesbian mom and five gender-neutral hand-me-down outfits and a box of generic diapers and NOTHING. SHE's the one stuck with ME. Feel sorry for HER!

MIKE. I don't feel sorry for her.

MAX. Why not?

MIKE. Because you really really love her.

>   (**MAX** *bawls.*)

I'm sorry.

MAX. I forgot my pain medication, that's all. I'm supposed to go every four hours and I think it's been eight.

MIKE. Are you in pain?

MAX. YES I'm in fucking pain.

>   (**MIKE** *goes to the counter. It is unstable.*)

MIKE. You need a new counter.

MAX. Shut UP.

MIKE. Colace?

MAX. That's constipation.

MIKE. Percocet.

MAX. *Percocet.*

MIKE. Acetaminophen plus oxycodone. Nice.

>   (*He pours water and shakes out a pill.*)

This is a really limited supply.

MAX. Right, why would I kill myself *now*?

>   (**MIKE** *hands* **MAX** *a pill. She breaks it and swallows half, hands the other half back.*)

MIKE. Take the whole thing.

MAX. It's bad for the baby.

MIKE. I think your doctor knows about the baby?

MAX. I need to stay alert.

MIKE. I hear you.

>   *(He swallows the other half of the pill.* **MAX** *stares.)*

My knee hurts.

MAX. Your *knee?*

MIKE. I had that tubing incident sophomore year?

>   *(***MIKE*** *swallows another pill.* **MAX** *glares.)*

MAX. Do you know what happened to me on Wednesday? This being Saturday? My uterus was pulled through an incision in my abdomen, sliced open around a live baby, stapled shut, and stuffed back in. I was hooked to a pain pump until yesterday, and I still haven't taken a shit. I don't want to hear about your sporting mishaps.

MIKE. I can get you more drugs.

MAX. Just respect, Mike.

>   *(***MIKE*** *looks at the baby. Melts.)*

MIKE. Wow.

MAX. She slept in my arm all night. At the hospital.

MIKE. They let you do that?

MAX. The day nurses don't. They're white and have sticks up their butts. But I asked the first night nurse who came to move her, "Can I keep my baby here?" She said, "You're the mommy. What you say go." I couldn't even sit up. I couldn't roll over. I had to ring the nurses to change her. But I could hold her. Right here. It was like: I can love you from a broken place. I can love you from whoever I am. I can take care of you from wherever, as whatever I am.

God that drug works fast. I think I'm gonna rest. We are going to rest.

MIKE. I'm sorry about my sister.

MAX. *(Trying to hold the bliss and calm.)* Could you just please never mention her fucking name in this house?

MIKE. I feel really bad.

MAX. You're not responsible.

MIKE. I was central to the project. I feel really bad.

MAX. Call your own mommy, okay?

MIKE. Do you like the travel system?

MAX. It was generous, Mike. Go in peace.

MIKE. Lisa feels really bad.

MAX. Um, what did I just say?

MIKE. She doesn't know I'm here. She wants to see the baby.

MAX. Ha ha.

MIKE. She, um... I came to tell you...

MAX. Lisa can make her own baby. She's got a whole sperm supply now, right?

MIKE. Actually she, um...

MAX. I haven't really slept the last three nights, and from what I hear I'm not gonna sleep much the next three years, so can you let us get some rest?

MIKE. Things aren't working out the way Lisa hoped.

MAX. How devastating.

MIKE. And...I am the dad.

MAX. So?

MIKE. Lisa says I have rights.

(Massive silence.)

MAX. Oh my god.

MIKE. Lisa wants a family, and she says this baby is family.

MAX. Oh my god.

MIKE. I thought you should know.

(Blackout.)

Scene Two

(Next day. **MAX** *sits with* **GOLDIE**, *who inspects the baby at* **MAX**'s *breast.* **GOLDIE** *is not much older than* **MAX**, *in a long skirt and a wig.)*

GOLDIE. She has the latch!

MAX. Good.

GOLDIE. Good for her, good for you. The kid's a champion. Aren't you, aren't you? You bore a beauty.

MAX. Thanks.

GOLDIE. She's doing her part, Maxine.

MAX. Just Max.

GOLDIE. See how your nipple is flat in her mouth, with her lower lip curved around the bottom; she's got this just right. I see some serious suck issues, and believe me, there is no suck issue here.

MAX. *(Genuine.)* Great. Ow!

GOLDIE. Sore, or violent searing pain?

MAX. Sore.

GOLDIE. Fine, sore is normal. Sore is, hello, you're a mommy.

MAX. My nipples are sore. The searing pain is everywhere else.

GOLDIE. How are your meds?

MAX. I stopped. I have to stay aware.

GOLDIE. There are no medals for courage in motherhood, Maxine.

MAX. My ex wants her.

GOLDIE. I saw the picture of you alone, but I didn't want to pry...

MAX. What do I do?

GOLDIE. It's good for a child to have a father. Maybe it didn't work out between the two of you, but if he's interested, why not consider some kind of a joint –

MAX. No, my ex. Lisa.

(*Micro-pause.*)

GOLDIE. You are facing complications I couldn't possibly understand. What shall we do for your milk?

MAX. What's wrong with me?

GOLDIE. You need to let down.

MAX. Oh, I have years to let her down.

GOLDIE. In my line of work there is an odious repetition of puns.

MAX. Sorry.

GOLDIE. Usually from fathers.

MAX. Well, I'm both.

GOLDIE. She needs both.

MAX. Good, because I am.

GOLDIE. Fine but for now you should please focus on being her mother, which is natural, no?

MAX. We are the most natural family in the world.

GOLDIE. Do us all a favor and don't make this infant a spokesperson for your marginal beliefs.

MAX. *My* marginal beliefs? How's that wig, in July?

GOLDIE. It's warm. Where is your support, Maxine?

MAX. I have four months unemployment, and then I look.

GOLDIE. Please tell me you understand the question.

MAX. It all happened so fast.

GOLDIE. I assume it happened at the usual speed. You can't do this all by yourself. Your parents are living?

MAX. Just my mother. She's coming next week.

GOLDIE. Good. Friends?

MAX. I'm still new to the city.

GOLDIE. If the father were in the picture he could make omelets and rub your feet.

MAX. Sounds great.

GOLDIE. Usually that's not what happens, so don't think you're missing anything. In this "progressive" neighborhood more likely he'd be taking up space on the couch, using the first person plural to brag about the birth. "We" pushed. "We" tore.

MAX. Goldie, do you have a problem with men?

GOLDIE. I have seven children.

MAX. Jesus.

GOLDIE. *(Dirty joke.)* How could I bear seven children if I had a problem with men? And yet, bearing seven children, how could I not have a tiny problem with men?

MAX. Does your husband discuss your body in the first person?

GOLDIE. My husband is a holy combatant for the chosen people.

MAX. Oh.

GOLDIE. The let down reflex is a miracle but it's not guaranteed. You must work for what God gave you.

MAX. I don't believe in God.

GOLDIE. I don't believe in single homosexual parenting. And yet you exist.

MAX. Help me.

GOLDIE. Would it be the worst thing to get the father involved?

MAX. The donor?

GOLDIE. Whatever you call him. Can you call him? Or was he in a tube?

MAX. He bought the travel system.

GOLDIE. Snugride, very nice. He has resources?

MAX. He's a drug dealer.

GOLDIE. Has he been caught?

MAX. Not yet.

GOLDIE. So he can help!

MAX. He's Lisa's brother.

GOLDIE. *(Shocked.)* No wonder she left you!

MAX. No, oh God no – we never... Lisa wanted to be related to our baby, so she and I talked, and talked, and talked, and finally we called Mike and he said yes right away. He even moved out here for the project. We decided, no doctors, no papers. At home, we would just –

GOLDIE. Okey dokey, no details.

MAX. You asked.

GOLDIE. Not exactly.

MAX. Well, you're here.

> *(Pause.)*

GOLDIE. Maxine, do you think there might be a reason why people do things the normal way?

MAX. I don't like that word.

GOLDIE. Good, because no one's ever going to use it about your child. In my community a new mother's feet don't touch the ground, there is so much support. Cooking, childcare, groceries. We're like a fence, bound together, strong in one another. You're more of a post. What good is one post?

MAX. Goodbye, Goldie. I'll bottle feed.

GOLDIE. Forgive me.

MAX. You are the only one here.

GOLDIE. Let me help you, Max. You and your little girl. I don't want you to give up on yourself. Give up on yourself and you give up on – who is this beauty?

MAX. Lakshmi Rose.

GOLDIE. *Who?*

MAX. Lakshmi was the Hindu goddess of love, fertility, and the lotus flower. And Rose...in case she needs an out.

GOLDIE. You're Hindu?

MAX. No, I like the concept.

GOLDIE. Do you want to give up on Lovey Rose?

MAX. Lakshmi.

GOLDIE. Do you want a mass-produced can of inverted corn syrup solids and hormone-injected dairy byproducts to mother Lovey Rose? Or do *you* want to mother Lovey Rose?

MAX. I want to mother Lovey Rose.

GOLDIE. Imagine waterfalls.

MAX. What?

GOLDIE. Close your eyes. A memory near a waterfall. Breathe.

MAX. Oh.

GOLDIE. You never saw a waterfall?

MAX. We backpacked through the Cascades.

GOLDIE. Washington State.

MAX. You've been?

GOLDIE. *(Present tense.)* I read.

MAX. Norse Peak. We climbed too high too early, past the snow line, lost the trail and built a fire. It was my idea to go so soon. I wanted the season to start.

GOLDIE. A fire in snow.

MAX. We sat by a lake all the next morning, fighting over how to get back. Then a dam of ice broke, and fresh water jumped straight down the face of the mountain. The lake started roaring, churning, it was spring.

> *(Closing her eyes.)*

Oh. Milk.

> *(She repositions the baby, who is completely quiet.)*

Thank you. Thank you, Goldie.

GOLDIE. Is this the face of God, or what?

MAX. Um...

GOLDIE. Head down, tushy up. You two are a team.

MAX. We are.

GOLDIE. For life, you two are a team.

MAX. Oh my god I've never been so happy.

GOLDIE. I'll make tea.

MAX. I should be making you...

GOLDIE. You should be waited upon like a queen. I'm going to make you one cup of tea while the *baybele* nurses so perfectly.

> (**GOLDIE** *goes to the stove. She gasps.)*

MAX. The back right burner works, it just needs a match.

GOLDIE. Didn't you *nest*?

MAX. We were gonna remodel...

GOLDIE. You have six months to get this place in shape, or move.

MAX. Please Goldie, I'm all let down.

GOLDIE. It is your job to create a sane world for this child.

MAX. If your God couldn't do that, how should I?

GOLDIE. Fix the stove.

MAX. I'm unemployed.

GOLDIE. Have you got a toothpick?

MAX. Probably not.

> (**GOLDIE** *finds a toothpick and cleans the burner.)*

GOLDIE. You are exhausted and overstressed. It affects your supply and will continue to do so. Someone needs to take care of you, Max, if you are going to feed this lotus rose.

MAX. Who takes care of you?

GOLDIE. My eldest, Shayna Brucha, a gift among gifts. Also God.

MAX. Maybe She has time for me. God. Your daughter sounds busy.

GOLDIE. Ladies and gentlemen, two burners.

MAX. How did you do that?

GOLDIE. I live rent controlled. No one fixes but me.

MAX. Thanks.

GOLDIE. *(Kind.)* It was recent you lost your father?

MAX. Five years.

GOLDIE. That's recent.

MAX. Thank you. Yeah.

GOLDIE. Imagine now: *you never had him.*

MAX. That's not fair. Mike is not an option. There's only...
Lisa.

GOLDIE. Lisa shmisa.

MAX. The project was her idea.

GOLDIE. Project? *Idea?* When you become a mother, you
become more animal, and also more divine. Idea has
nothing to do with it.

MAX. My politics suggest otherwise.

GOLDIE. Will your politics love you back? Look, this one
already knows who's mommy. You are her heaven and
her earth. Your breast is her sun and moon and stars.
Enjoy.

MAX. You'll come back tomorrow, right?

GOLDIE. It would be taking advantage.

MAX. What if I can't nurse without you?

GOLDIE. Your body knows what to do.

MAX. I thought this was a relationship.

GOLDIE. I'll follow up by phone.

MAX. How do I protect her?

GOLDIE. Maxine. In your many outdoor expeditions, did you ever see a mother bear with cubs?

MAX. Once I saw cubs.

GOLDIE. And?

MAX. We backed up and cancelled the hike.

GOLDIE. Learn from the rest of God's realm.

>   *(Tea kettle whistles.)*

How do you take it?

MAX. I'll wait actually; I don't want to burn her.

GOLDIE. You see? You already know.

MAX. *(Closing her eyes.)* This is really good.

GOLDIE. Bliss. The body releases waves of bliss.

>   *(They sit together for a sweet moment.)*

One-seventy-five.

Scene Three

(A few days later, the empty apartment. **MAX** *enters wheeling a small grocery cart, with Lakshmi in the sling.* **MAX** *is drinking a smoothie, looking a little better. She takes groceries out of the suitcase, with some effort.)*

MAX. Vitamins. Yogurt. Water filters. Baby, we are on the rise. Napping? Napping like the contented little milked-up eight-day-old molecule you are? Mommy's going to sleep too, one of these nights, and then we'll be all –

(A crash from offstage.)

Who's there?

*(***MAX*** *grabs a butter knife, hyperventilating.)*

You picked the wrong house, motherfucker! I got a baby. I got a knife. I am in prime fighting condition!

*(***LISA*** *enters from the bedroom. Around Max's age, corporate chic.)*

LISA. Hey, Max.

MAX. You don't live here!

LISA. I used my key.

MAX. I'm changing the locks!

LISA. That's kind of extreme.

MAX. Extreme? Extreme? Lisa, your behavior is extreme. Yours! You don't live here. You "couldn't" live here. You. **You Lisa you!**

LISA. You asked me to get my things.

MAX. Four months ago! I did not ask you to sneak unannounced into the home where my daughter and I –

LISA. Stay calm.

MAX. **Calm?** You filled a syringe with your brother's semen, expelled it into my vagina, then left me pregnant, with a mortgage, unemployed –

LISA. That happened earlier –

MAX. – so you could more freely fuck your boss. The man who offered you that miracle goddamn job in the first place, bringing us to this lunar landscape where I can't plant a tomato in dirt without paying nine hundred bucks for a lead inspection –

LISA. Get the inspection; send me the tab.

MAX. It's too late in *summer*, do we not occupy the same *planet*?

LISA. I don't know, Max. I buy tomatoes at the store.

MAX. Me too, now. Thanks a lot! Twelve years of gardening and I buy spongy red bullshit wrapped in cellophane from the store!

LISA. I just said I'd *pay* for the *inspection*.

MAX. And I just said *it's too late!*

> *(Beat.)*

Why are we talking about tomatoes? You do this. You twist things.

LISA. You brought it up.

MAX. I did not. Did I?

LISA. Mmm –

MAX. Yes I did! I was saying! How after breaking big promises, lifetime promises, you made a crappy little promise to clear out your belongings, then failed to do even that, leaving my home clogged with your athletic gear, legal briefs, and winter coats, up to and through the delivery of this child!

LISA. That's why I'm here.

MAX. That's all?

LISA. Whatever you need.

MAX. Get your things and go.

LISA. Here's my key. Save your money.

MAX. Thanks.

LISA. *(Fond memory.)* Remember how those Israeli locksmith bastards ripped us off the first time?

MAX. Shut up, you bigot.

LISA. Umm...

MAX. The Jews have had to struggle. No wonder they overcharge.

LISA. We both live with the fallout, Max.

MAX. No. This is not a joint experience. No. You were "falling into your true self," "exploring mature love," stroke by keystroke. I just happened to –

LISA. You just happened to load spy software onto my laptop?

MAX. I was provoked.

LISA. How?

MAX. You changed your password.

LISA. Why were you reading my e-mail?

MAX. I didn't read your e-mail, Lisa! I just sometimes used to check who it was from.

LISA. Can I meet the baby?

MAX. She's asleep.

(*But she lets* **LISA** *peek into the sling.*)

LISA. Oh my god.

MAX. Right?

LISA. What's her name?

MAX. Lakshmi Rose.

LISA. That's perfect.

MAX. Thanks.

LISA. You give her the power, the grace, of a goddess. And then you give her the out.

MAX. Exactly.

LISA. And the last name?

MAX. She has my last name.

LISA. Right.

MAX. Obviously.

LISA. We'd talked about the hyphen –

MAX. No hyphen. My name.

LISA. Well, thanks for the "L." What an honor.

*(Pause as **MAX** connects the two "L" names.)*

MAX. Get the fuck out of here, Lisa.

LISA. I pay mortgage.

MAX. Not half.

LISA. It was my down payment.

MAX. From your signing bonus.

LISA. I'm a manifester.

MAX. Manifest a man with a van. I want to set up a nursery in there.

LISA. Did you order baby furniture?

MAX. She needs a space.

LISA. She can't even see.

MAX. Yes she can.

LISA. Not till six weeks. I bought a book.

MAX. She can see!

LISA. Short distances.

MAX. She can see furniture!

LISA. She doesn't have furniture.

MAX. What are you doing here? Peeing? Peeing all over my place?

LISA. Eww. I thought you might need help. I could measure the room. Bring you catalogues. It could be beautiful. The bones are all there.

MAX. Yes they are.

LISA. She deserves a perfect start.

MAX. She does.

LISA. All possible support.

MAX. Shut up.

LISA. You're going to be a great mom, Max. Lakshmi Rose is truly fortunate.

(**MAX** *growls like a bear.*)

Does it bother you for her to be exposed to your anger?

MAX. She's asleep.

LISA. All those nights your mom and dad thought you were asleep, were you?

MAX. She is eight days old. I can see her. Asleep.

LISA. The subconscious forms early. Earlier than we knew. But you'll figure it out. The floor, the finances...

MAX. She's not your baby.

LISA. *(Addressing off.)* Come on in.

> *(***MIKE*** *enters sheepishly, carrying an unwieldy
> load of Lisa's stuff.)*

MAX. Who the hell else is back there?

LISA. Just family.

MIKE. I wasn't listening. I don't get up in other people's business. Not that I know anyone who does. Not that that's a subject under discussion.

LISA. Mike, meet Lakshmi. Isn't that a beautiful name?

MAX. Yeah, Mike. Let me introduce you.

LISA. You made her. You two. Wow!

> *(***LISA*** *exits, towards her stuff.* ***MIKE*** *slips* ***MAX***
> *a large vial of pills.)*

MIKE. Restock.

MAX. I don't want your dirty drugs.

MIKE. Clean drugs. Prescription. It's strong so go slow. Peace.

MAX. No justice, no peace, you craven asshole.

> *(***MAX*** *leaves the bottle on the counter.* ***LISA***
> *enters with a personal item and puts it on top
> of* ***MIKE****'s pile.)*

LISA. She's got your chin, huh Mikey?

MIKE. She has no chin at all.

LISA. Exactly.

(To ***MAX****.)* Do you want me to stay? Because I would consider that.

> *(***MAX*** *growls like a bear.)*

Kay. We'll be back.

MAX. No...

LISA. Enjoy.

> (**LISA** *and* **MIKE** *leave,* **LISA** *carrying nothing.*)

> (**MAX** *punches the countertop. It collapses, spilling the groceries, while she doubles over in pain from her incision.*)

> (*On the floor,* **MAX** *growls. The baby cries. Max's phone rings.*)

MAX. NO!

> (**MAX** *picks up the baby and half-crawls, half-scoots to her phone. She hits speaker.*)

GOLDIE'S VOICE. Maxine? Max?

MAX. Hi.

GOLDIE'S VOICE. This is Goldie Friedenthaler, following up.

MAX. Goldie.

GOLDIE'S VOICE. How's the lotus goddess?

MAX. Goldie, can you come over?

GOLDIE'S VOICE. What's going on?

MAX. There's no one.

GOLDIE'S VOICE. The milk?

MAX. The milk isn't the same.

GOLDIE'S VOICE. You have milk?

MAX. Not enough, I don't think.

GOLDIE'S VOICE. Your breasts are drained after you nurse?

MAX. Everything is drained...

GOLDIE'S VOICE. Milk in the corners of her mouth?

MAX. When do *I* get to nurse?

GOLDIE'S VOICE. We must have a bad connection.

MAX. Who holds *me*?

GOLDIE'S VOICE. It sounds like the baby is thriving.

MAX. I'm going to break her.

GOLDIE'S VOICE. These first weeks are very difficult…

MAX. I'm in pain.

GOLDIE'S VOICE. Your nipples are round when she's done?

MAX. Goldie, I'm in pain.

GOLDIE'S VOICE. I am following up about your milk.

MAX. This poor perfect baby cursed with me for a mother.
This poor perfect baby.

> (**MAX** *hangs up and cries. She talks to the baby.*)

I want you to know in advance that I am sorry. When
you grow up and have a fixed craving for nurturance,
when you marry someone twice your age who appears
to provide solidity but actually wants to crush your
soul, when you mistake rigidity for sanity, that is my
fault.

After you were born I was alone and somewhat out of
my mind, and I was unresponsive to your demands.
I was inconsistent. I had never been flighty, never
wanted to go anyplace at all really; I thought stability
would be my forte as a mom, but then, after you were
born –

> (**MAX** *puppets the baby, a nightmare teen.*)

(*As baby/teen.*) "I'm engaged to my math teacher!"

(*As* **MAX**.) That's my fault.

MAX. *(As baby/teen.)* "We're happy Mom! We're in love! We solve equations!"

(As **MAX**, *more desperate.)* I'm sorry you think that's happiness. It's my fault.

(As baby/teen, super happy.) "Well, thanks. Thanks for being so shitty. Now I know shitty shitty love!"

(As **MAX**.*)* You're engaged to your math teacher?

(As baby/teen.) "He smells good. Like chalk. Like the answer."

(As **MAX**.*)* I'm sorry I wasn't gravity, I'm sorry I didn't pull hard enough, I'm sorry –

(As baby/teen.) "Volume of a cone, mom! Volume of a sphere!"

(As **MAX**.*)* Are you **pregnant?!?**

> *(***MAX*** marginally regains her senses.)*

Dammit Goldie! Why don't you call us back?

> *(***MAX*** calls* **GOLDIE**. *This time we might see* **GOLDIE** *answer in her office. Images of nursing in painting and popular culture, pictures of breasts everywhere.)*

GOLDIE. Hello?

MAX. I need you.

GOLDIE. Please explain the problem.

MAX. I can't let down. I'm very tense.

GOLDIE. And the Buddha?

MAX. She's in danger.

GOLDIE. I don't hear her.

MAX. She's lost her voice.

GOLDIE. See the pediatrician.

MAX. Metaphorically, she lost her voice.

GOLDIE. This is a week-old baby, she makes a sound or she doesn't.

MAX. I just saw her as a young woman.

GOLDIE. How beautiful.

MAX. No! I got her into this mess, and it's going to take her eighty years to get out.

GOLDIE. What mess?

MAX. Life.

GOLDIE. When does your mother arrive?

MAX. She's not coming.

GOLDIE. She *what*?

MAX. She called. She's busy.

GOLDIE. This is her grandchild. You are her child.

MAX. I know who everybody is, okay Goldie?

GOLDIE. Poor baby.

MAX. I know. She gets knocked up by some faculty lounge scum. She's never going to have time for therapy, for drugs, all the wonderful ways I spent my youth.

GOLDIE. I mean you.

MAX. Me?

GOLDIE. The baby is a baby.

MAX. Are you sure?

GOLDIE. Check.

> (**MAX** *looks at infant Lakshmi, relaxes a little.*)

MAX. She's a baby.

GOLDIE. What are you eating?

MAX. I bought groceries; yogurt and broccoli.

GOLDIE. Fine, if you eat what you bought. How's your fluid intake?

MAX. *(Lying.)* Gallon a day?

GOLDIE. Do you sleep?

MAX. I have nightmares.

GOLDIE. Good, that means you're asleep.

MAX. I can't sleep, because of the nightmares.

GOLDIE. You need to sleep, and to eat.

MAX. Tell me about waterfalls.

GOLDIE. You tell me. I only see the one in Prospect Park.

MAX. I once walked the whole state of Washington.

GOLDIE. I didn't know a person could do that.

MAX. We watched the world melt. Spring into summer. Moving north, the season changed slowly, with us, larkspur until August. And then the fall came fast; we walked right into winter, leaves gold one day, red the next, bare branches within a week. We arrived in October, at the first snow.

GOLDIE. Snow to snow. I can't imagine.

MAX. You never camped?

GOLDIE. We get a cabin in the Catskills a couple weeks, summers.

MAX. I'll take you.

GOLDIE. Maxine.

MAX. And the family.

GOLDIE. Hiking boots for nine? That would make the shoe man happy.

MAX. You have a way with natural things.

GOLDIE. I would like to see an animal that nobody owns.

MAX. Milk.

> (**MAX** *looks at Lakshmi, but doesn't nurse.*)

GOLDIE. Head down, tushy up.

MAX. I know. Or she knows.

GOLDIE. She's a beauty.

MAX. She's very small, right?

GOLDIE. She's going to be small for a long time.

MAX. She's not even going to be able to crawl for a long time.

GOLDIE. You'd better hope not, with those floors.

MAX. And then, I can block the door.

GOLDIE. There are safety latches.

MAX. I can latch her in.

GOLDIE. I worry about you.

MAX. The milk is flowing. You did great.

GOLDIE. Can your mother change her –

MAX. My mother doesn't change.

GOLDIE. You need someone –

> (**MAX** *hangs up the phone. Lights out on* **MAX**, *leaving* **GOLDIE** *alone in her space.*)

Who do you think you are? A baby and no stove? No help? You think you're an exception to natural laws?

WHAT THE HELL WERE YOU THINKING, YOU ARROGANT DYKE?

(A flat **TEENAGE GIRL***'s voice, off.)*

SHAYNA. *(Offstage.)* It's just work, Ma. Don't take it so personal.

(Lights out on **GOLDIE***.)*

Scene Four

(Late the next night.)

*(**MAX** stands at the door with **SHAYNA BRUCHA**, a low-affect teenager in a long denim skirt and high top sneakers.)*

SHAYNA. My mother sent me. Mrs. Friedenthaler.

MAX. So late?

SHAYNA. She couldn't spare me any earlier. I'm invaluable. It's a mitzvah to visit the sick.

MAX. Am I sick?

SHAYNA. I brought you a kugel.

MAX. Thanks.

SHAYNA. Is it true you're a lesbian with no help?

MAX. Um –

SHAYNA. Not that I care.

MAX. Do you want to see the baby?

SHAYNA. Hello, I see babies all day? Home office?

MAX. Right, plus you have all those siblings.

SHAYNA. Just six.

MAX. Just six. Do you want tea, or some juice?

SHAYNA. You're not kosher but I can have a glass of water.

MAX. Okay.

SHAYNA. I'll help myself. You heal. Can I put this in the fridge?

MAX. That was very sweet of your mother.

SHAYNA. She feels sorry for you, without a husband or God or anything.

MAX. I'm very happy.

SHAYNA. How could you be happy? With all that you lack?

MAX. How can you be happy without R-rated movies or pants?

SHAYNA. I'm not happy.

MAX. It was nice of your mother to send the food.

SHAYNA. You can throw out the dish.

MAX. Why would I do that?

SHAYNA. Or keep it; it's good, but we don't want it back. We can't use it once it's been here. How's your milk supply?

MAX. She eats a lot.

SHAYNA. Does it hurt?

MAX. Yes.

SHAYNA. I knew they lie.

MAX. It doesn't hurt everyone.

SHAYNA. Like, who doesn't it hurt?

MAX. I don't know every woman.

SHAYNA. But you sure know some.

(**SHAYNA** *giggles.*)

MAX. Why didn't Goldie come herself?

SHAYNA. She doesn't want to charge you, and she doesn't want to be your friend.

MAX. Ah.

SHAYNA. My time is obviously less valuable, so give me twenty bucks and we're good.

MAX. Shall I call her to check on that?

SHAYNA. Ha ha. Like I said, it's a mitzvah. Eternal life is all I care about. That, and healing the world.

(Baby cries. **MAX** *turns to attend to her.* **SHAYNA** *pockets the bottle of pills* **MIKE** *left on the counter.)*

MAX. Come to Mama, Lakshmi Rose.

*(***MAX*** *holds the baby, who quiets down.)*

SHAYNA. Wow, you act like a normal mother.

MAX. I am a normal mother.

SHAYNA. I don't think you're arrogant, or selfish, necessarily.

MAX. What did Goldie say about me?

SHAYNA. I mean, if no one loves you and your homosexual lifestyle isn't helping, maybe you have to manufacture a family. At least you did this locally and not imported. My mom sees all kinds of weirdos. People who like won't buy a cantaloupe from Mexico but then fly to Ethiopia to get a kid. Tuck her arm under so she can get closer to your nipple.

MAX. Thank your mother from me.

SHAYNA. I don't have to go home right away.

MAX. Well, sit and drink your water if you want.

*(***SHAYNA*** *drinks her water, looking around.)*

SHAYNA. What happened to this place?

MAX. It's old.

SHAYNA. All the buildings around here are old, but they don't look like this.

MAX. Well, no one took care of it, so it was cheaper to buy. The idea was we could restore it.

SHAYNA. That worked.

MAX. We can sell.

SHAYNA. Is that what lesbians do? Buy broken things and make them better?

MAX. Some, I guess.

SHAYNA. But then some fall down on the job, like you?

MAX. There are lots of kinds of lesbians. Home builders, apartment dwellers, movie stars...

SHAYNA. Not movie stars.

MAX. Oh yes.

SHAYNA. Do you have any books on it?

MAX. Home repair?

(**SHAYNA** *looks at* **MAX,** *beseechingly.*)

Oh. Oh, honey.

SHAYNA. Do you like me?

MAX. I – you seem like a really dynamic girl.

SHAYNA. Will anyone ever like me?

MAX. Listen. Listen to me... remind me your name?

SHAYNA. I hate my name.

MAX. Shayna?

SHAYNA. Shayna Brucha. Beautiful blessing. Some joke.

MAX. It's not a joke. You will find love, Shayna Brucha.

SHAYNA. You didn't.

MAX. I did, for many years.

SHAYNA. But now you're alone and there's a hole in your house.

MAX. It's fixable.

SHAYNA. Will you fix it?

MAX. Yes I will.

SHAYNA. Do you want to have relations?

MAX. I can't do that.

SHAYNA. I'm a quick study.

MAX. It's not personal.

SHAYNA. Okay bye.

*(**SHAYNA** heads for the door.)*

MAX. You have a long road, I'm not going to lie. But there will be beautiful stretches on that road, beautiful blessings –

(Loud banging outside the door.)

LISA. *(A wild mess. Offstage.)* **I AM DROWNING WITHOUT YOU!**

MAX. **FUCK OFF, LISA!**

SHAYNA. Is that *her*?

(Pounding on the door continues.)

MAX. There are many ways to live a life. You see only one model now, where you're growing up, but there are many many ways to be happy. There are so many kinds of family.

LISA. **OPEN THE DOOR!**

MAX. **GET AWAY FROM MY HOUSE!**

LISA. **JOINT TENANTS WITH RIGHT OF SURVIVORSHIP, BABY!**

SHAYNA. Is Lisa pretty?

MAX. Sit down.

SHAYNA. I want to see her.

MAX. Don't open that door.

> *(Max's phone rings.)*

(Into the phone.) I'm not talking to you.

> *(We hear* **LISA** *through the door, but* **MAX** *talks into the phone.)*

LISA. I've become unmoored.

MAX. The guy is married, Lisa. Do the math.

LISA. I'm so confused.

MAX. This is not a confusing situation. You're evil, your boss is evil, the rest of us are somewhere on the good-bad continuum.

> *(***MAX*** hangs up, but* **LISA** *continues to moan through the door.)*

LISA. **IF I'M EVIL, HOW DID YOU LOVE ME SO LONG?**

SHAYNA. Good question.

LISA. **I SUPPORTED YOU THROUGH SCHOOL.**

MAX. **I TOOK LOANS.**

LISA. **EMOTIONALLY. I SUPPORTED YOU EMOTIONALLY.**

MAX. I'm calling the cops!

LISA. **PLEASE MAX PLEASE! LET ME IN, JUST TO TALK.**

MAX. **LAKSHMI IS SLEEPING.** Shh!

LISA. I'll sleep too! We can all just snuggle with that crib thingy you set up by the bed, and not say a word!

SHAYNA. That sounds nice.

MAX. *(To* **LISA**.*)* Go home!

LISA. **YOU WERE MY HOME AND NOW YOU'RE GONE.**

MAX. What happened since yesterday?

LISA. **I WANT TO DIE.**

MAX. Don't die, Lisa, just get very far from me. Goodnight.

> *(A key turns in the lock.)*

What the hell –

> *(***LISA*** enters, calm.)*

LISA. I had a spare.

SHAYNA. How romantic.

MAX. My dreams of killing you are very vivid.

LISA. Who's she?

SHAYNA. Call me Shay.

MAX. She brought kugel. She's going home.

LISA. Who do you know who makes kugel?

SHAYNA. You might not want to eat the kugel; it was kind of an experiment.

MAX. Does your mother even know you're here?

LISA. Run along, pious person. Take your food.

SHAYNA. It's too late.

MAX. She can't use the dish.

LISA. This is family time.

SHAYNA. I want to stay and see many kinds of family.

MAX. No one is staying. Lakshmi needs a diaper change and –

SHAYNA. I'll do it.

MAX. You don't know –

SHAYNA. I've changed a lot more diapers than you.

(**SHAYNA** *exits, expertly holding Lakshmi.*)

LISA. You're beautiful. Even all puffy.

MAX. Did you not leave me?

LISA. The best I ever was, was with you. Together we had a chance for purity. You saw good in me, Max.

MAX. I was mistaken.

LISA. I love you.

MAX. I'm calling Mike.

LISA. He's a twenty-four-year-old drug dealer. Don't get him involved.

MAX. I think he's involved, Lisa. It was his sperm!

SHAYNA. *(Offstage.)* Oh wow.

LISA. I'll make you some tea.

MAX. No.

LISA. Herbal. It'll calm you.

MAX. You know what would calm me? New locks.

LISA. I'll call the guys right now. Avi and Avi?

MAX. I'll call when you're gone. Both of you.

(**SHAYNA** *enters, sets Lakshmi in her Snugride seat.*)

LISA. *(To* **SHAYNA**.*)* Tea?

MAX. She can't.

SHAYNA. Yes, please!

LISA. Wow, the burner works.

MAX. Goldie.

LISA. Who's Goldie?

SHAYNA. My mom. Would you say that you're miserable because you're an aberration in the eyes of God, or vice versa?

LISA. What are you talking about? I'm a happy person.

SHAYNA. You screamed you were drowning.

LISA. That was then. Now I'm good.

SHAYNA. Sometimes I think I'm drowning.

MAX. Go home, Shayna Brucha.

SHAYNA. Let me stay?

MAX. Go directly home, and do whatever you can to avoid ending up like us.

SHAYNA. Please?

MAX. No.

SHAYNA. Okay.

(**SHAYNA** *slips out the door.*)

LISA. So gay.

MAX. I know.

LISA. How's that gonna work?

MAX. Right?

LISA. God I love this house. The potential. I still imagine the sky blue ceiling, silver molding. You've got the eye; I make it happen.

MAX. That was us.

LISA. How are you feeling?

MAX. Physically?

LISA. Anything.

MAX. I can't believe I ever didn't know her.

LISA. Is it hard?

MAX. Is love hard?

LISA. Yeah.

MAX. So it's like loving a person who happens to have no ability to care for herself. Not entirely unfamiliar.

LISA. He asked me to marry him.

MAX. Congratulations.

LISA. I don't think I'm a wife.

MAX. Which requirement concerns you? Generosity? Fidelity? Kindness?

LISA. I liked being queer.

MAX. You can't use that word.

LISA. Who cares what words we use? What we call things?

MAX. "We" have leeway. You don't, anymore.

LISA. I shower at work, Max. The days his daughters come. I keep little Kiehls samples at work.

MAX. Isn't that why corporate offices have showers? So you bloodsuckers can wreck each other's lives and not stink at meetings?

LISA. It's like he speaks a different language.

MAX. Check the self-help section. It's full of books for women about how to talk to men. None needed for women about talking to women, why do you think that is? But maybe I'll write one. Maybe that'll be my big life thing to do: "When Venus Seeks a Penis: a Survival Guide."

LISA. You're so funny.

MAX. Yeah, well.

LISA. Do you think you'll move back to Portland? After we sell?

MAX. Oh, are you finally ready to sell?

LISA. This market is no time for sudden moves.

MAX. You made a sudden move.

>   *(Beat.)*

Portland could be great. I just need to settle in with Lakshmi before I decide anything else. I need a little time without change.

LISA. Didn't we have fifteen years without change?

MAX. I didn't see it that way.

LISA. Me neither.

MAX. I thought we were stable in a good sense. Until you went all alpha and biologicial.

LISA. It's so ironic if it was biological, because the baby is here.

MAX. I told you that four months ago.

LISA. I want you back.

>   *(**MAX** grabs the picture of herself from the mantle and gives it to **LISA**.)*

MAX. Pray to it.

LISA. Norse Peak. Lupine in your hair.

MAX. It was in the background.

LISA. It looks like it's growing out of your hair.

MAX. I know.

LISA. We were happy.

MAX. We were twenty.

LISA. *(Of photo.)* Was that before or after the bear?

MAX. Before, are you kidding? Look how calm I am.

LISA. Right, afterwards we were basically scrambling to the lodge.

MAX. *(Sexy memory.)* The lodge.

LISA. Last minute check-in. All our cash. Did we even have credit cards yet?

MAX. I don't think so.

LISA. You were so sure of yourself. The gear, the maps.

MAX. You caught on.

LISA. When you start out early, you can go anywhere.

MAX. That's what I tried to tell you –

> (**LISA** *kisses* **MAX**. **MAX** *returns the kiss, then pulls back.*)

I'm really off here, Lisa.

LISA. I'm sorry.

MAX. Please go.

LISA. Of course.

MAX. Leave me your key. Again.

LISA. Your feet must be sore.

MAX. Yeah.

LISA. You carry so much.

MAX. I do.

LISA. Could I help you? Could I rub them?

MAX. Umm...

LISA. What?

MAX. It's been so long since anyone…

LISA. Just feet.

MAX. You know my feet.

LISA. I do.

> (**LISA** *slips off* **MAX**'s *shoes and rubs her feet.*)

MAX. Oh.

LISA. Shhh.

MAX. *(Alert for a moment.)* Promise you'll leave as soon
as I –

LISA. I promise.

MAX. I'm just so, so tir…

> (**MAX** *drifts off to sleep as* **LISA** *rubs her feet.*)

LISA. Shh. Shh.

> (**LISA** *sits cradling* **MAX**'s *feet a while.*)

Shh. Shh.

> (**LISA** *sets her house key on the table and
> tucks a blanket around* **MAX**'s *feet. She kneels
> on the floor next to the Snugride with Baby
> Lakshmi in it.*)

There is so much love around you. So much love.

> (*Gently, swiftly,* **LISA** *lifts the Snugride and
> carries the baby out into the night.*)

> (**MAX** *sleeps.*)

End of Act One

ACT TWO

Scene One

(A curtained area in a Brooklyn emergency room. **SHAYNA** *lies in a hospital bed, unconscious.* **GOLDIE** *sits holding* **SHAYNA**'s *hand, reading a tiny book of Yiddish prayers.* **GOLDIE**'s *lips move quickly but she barely makes a sound.)*

*(**MIKE** enters, hovers.)*

GOLDIE. Wrong room.

MIKE. Are you Goldie?

*(**GOLDIE** nods.)*

I think your daughter took a lot of these.

*(He hands **GOLDIE** a pill.)*

GOLDIE. Who are you?

MIKE. I'm...the supply guy.

GOLDIE. Dr. McDoobie?

MIKE. That's um. I'm afraid that's not my real name.

GOLDIE. You're the number on the bottle.

MIKE. Yeah.

GOLDIE. **You pushed drugs at my daughter!**

MIKE. No, she um – My um – She would have got them from Max.

GOLDIE. **Max pushed drugs at my daughter?!**

MIKE. Max would never! Um, my name is Mike.

GOLDIE. The father.

MIKE. Ah, not our term, but...

GOLDIE. Mr. Squirt and Desert!

MIKE. This is Vicodin, acetaminophen plus hydrocodone. She needs a medicine called Narcan, to block the opiates? Also something to control liver damage.

GOLDIE. They're running tests.

MIKE. To see what she took. But I'm telling you what she took.

GOLDIE. Why would she?

MIKE. I never met your daughter.

GOLDIE. A gift among gifts. Knows my kids better than I do. Because of Shayna Brucha I can support this family. A top student. Sullen sometimes, she likes her privacy, but this?

MIKE. Um – time can be a factor here.

> (**GOLDIE** *grabs the pill from* **MIKE***'s hand and runs out of the room.* **MIKE** *tries to pray from Goldie's book, but it's in Yiddish.*)

What the fuck?

> (*He paces the tiny space.*)

Mike did not ask to bring life. Mike did not ask to bring – All Mike asks is to make his way with grace.

(*To* **SHAYNA**.) You little thief. Those were for Max. For her pain.

If you wake up I promise I will get you one of anything you ask. I swear. High of your choice, gratis. Once. I'm not a fucking pusher. I sell to owners of condos and townhomes.

Yo, we all have our days, little one, where it looks like it could be a better option to just not. I had some days like that, for sure. But you know if you listen to those days, how are you gonna get to the other days?

Girls? You want girls? You want in on that complicated baby lesbian life? I will hook you up. You just rise and receive.

    *(**GOLDIE** enters.)*

GOLDIE. They're coming.

MIKE. Awesome.

GOLDIE. The nurse said I could stay, or step out.

MIKE. She's gonna puke, and shit, and sweat, and scream.

GOLDIE. And wake up?

MIKE. Hopefully.

GOLDIE. We'll stay.

    *(Just as they settle in, **MAX** enters – unhinged,*
    *a hiking-style headlamp on her head. **MAX** is*
    about to blurt something out, but stops at the
    sight.)

MAX. Shayna. Goldie. Oh poor Shayna. How is she –

GOLDIE. **What was my daughter doing at your house?**

    *(**MAX** and **GOLDIE** regard each other.)*

MIKE. Max is searching for Lakshmi.

GOLDIE. The *baby*?

MIKE. My sister borrowed her.

GOLDIE. What is the matter with your family?

Forget it. They have a medication.

MAX. Good. Goldie, I wish I could –

GOLDIE. I said forget it. Find your Buddha.

MAX. I'll come back.

GOLDIE. Don't bother. You give your child a ridiculous name because you *like the concept*? A child is not a concept. A child is a separate human person with the breath of God. I work at my marriage. I work for my family. You think it's a science project, mix it up in a cup and see what you get? Isaac says Goldie, you have to draw a line with these people and from now on, I draw. Enough is enough.

MAX. I'm very sorry about Shayna.

(**MAX** *and* **MIKE** *step out...*)

Scene Two

(...and **MAX** *pulls* **MIKE** *into a hospital corridor.)*

MAX. WHERE IS MY BABY YOU MOTHERFUCKER?!

MIKE. Chill.

MAX. I WILL CHILL WHEN I SEE MY BABY YOU MOTHERFUCKER!

MIKE. And get that thing off your head; this isn't the goddamn woods.

*(***MAX*** removes the headlamp.)*

Now lower your voice. There's heaviness here for a lot of people.

MAX. There's going to be heaviness on YOU if you do not take me to the lying bitch who stole my baby.

MIKE. I don't know where they are.

MAX. Bullshit.

MIKE. But Lakshmi Rose will be safe.

MAX. What does that mean?

MIKE. No harm will come.

MAX. You talked to Lisa?

MIKE. Not recently.

MAX. Where is she?

MIKE. *(The truth.)* I swear I don't know.

MAX. Lakshmi eats every ninety minutes! It has been way more than ninety minutes.

MIKE. Lisa will work that out.

MAX. Who is Lisa, your boss? Your God?

MIKE. She's my sister.

MAX. She is a deceitful, heart-sucking, emotionally abusive criminal.

MIKE. I know that.

MAX. So why do you trust her?

MIKE. Lisa is confused and upset.

MAX. Upset? Up-fucking-*set*?

MIKE. Lisa wants time with the baby. She wants to bond. She wouldn't steal her to another country / or anything.

MAX. Another / *country*?

MIKE. Lisa is lonely. She pushes away people who she loves. But, I'm her brother, so it doesn't work as well.

MAX. Rise up, Mike.

MIKE. And do what you want instead?

MAX. WHERE IS MY BABY?

(**MAX** *notices milk stains on her shirt.*)

Milk. Great. Everywhere. Perfect.

MIKE. That's a good sign, right? You think about her and make milk?

MAX. I'm exploding. My boobs are like rocks. I need that baby.

MIKE. Maybe Lisa was considering Lakshmi Rose, in all of this.

MAX. Come again?

MIKE. You are unstable. Everything about your house is falling down, even the counter. You don't have a job.

MAX. You don't have a job.

MIKE. I have income.

MAX. From dangerous chemicals that sent a teenager into a coma.

(**MIKE** *panics.*)

MIKE. What if she dies?

MAX. Don't *you* start.

MIKE. I felt so bad that I swallowed your pills, and then I hid in your house with Lisa, even though it was to get her stuff, which I thought you wanted gone. I felt so bad thinking about you with all that pain. I got you a refill to put things right.

MAX. Where is / Lisa.

MIKE. I thought you guys were forever! That ceremony in Hawaii? I kept the pictures. Max, when we met I was shorter than you. I would not have signed on to this project had I understood the volatility of your bond.

MAX. Me neither.

MIKE. I've got to think more like a chess player. What's the other guy's next move? I barely know my own next move. It does not make me competitive in this world.

MAX. Mike –

MIKE. Lisa thinks like a chess player.

MAX. Yeah. We've played chess.

MIKE. My condolences.

MAX. Where is she?

MIKE. Was it wrong to agree to the project?

MAX. What?

MIKE. To sire a baby under suboptimal conditions?

MAX. Nothing that made Lakshmi was wrong.

MIKE. But look at the pain I caused. Vials and vials of pain.

MAX. Mike, if you're looking at the pain you're looking through your ass.

I was with my dad at the end, right?

MIKE. I remember.

MAX. And those last couple days he couldn't talk. He couldn't move. He could see a little less, and then a little less. But it was him. It was one hundred percent him. And then we went in one morning, and it was not him at all, and I saw firsthand, people do not fade out. They are a hundred percent there, until they are not.

But I didn't know this, firsthand, about the beginning of life, until Lakshmi. I couldn't move my arms after the c-section, Mike. The nurse had to hold her to me. But I could feel – I can feel – when I am with her, that she is here. One hundred percent. She has arrived.

I don't believe in God.

MIKE. I know that.

MAX. But this is objective. I believe in the soul. I have seen it go out. I have seen it come in. When I hold her, I am cradling a human soul. She doesn't even know I'm separate from her. Can you imagine?

MIKE. Lakshmi Rose is unaware that she ends and you begin.

MAX. And yet it was possible for someone to tear her from me. Like it would be possible to tear out an eye. Or your dick.

MIKE. Don't hurt me.

MAX. Find me your fucking sister.

Scene Three

(A masculine executive office in a posh Manhattan law firm, later the same night.)

*(**LISA** sits on the desk with the baby carrier, trying to feed the baby a bottle without taking her out of the carrier. Lakshmi Rose is screaming.)*

LISA. Eat. Eat something. Would you eat?

Hey! I made a purchase!

*(**LISA** plays an inane children's lullaby from her phone.* It has no effect.)*

Nice, right?

*(**LISA** hums along, becoming a little calmer herself.)*

Once upon a time, there were two mommies. Only they weren't mommies yet. They had just barely finished being girls, walking and playing in the woods. The mommies lived in a little house with a purple door and a bathtub outside, and they grew their own grapes, and tomatoes, and squash. Well, one of the mommies did most of the growing. We'll call her Max. Mommy Max would fetch organic chicken poop from a farm, to spread on her plants, and she'd wear overalls with her hair under a cap, like a boy from olden times, but she never looked like a boy. She looked like a princess in disguise. And the other mommy, let's call her Lisa, would drink coffee on the porch next to the outdoor tub, and read about the history and the future of justice. The mommies passed many days in this way, many seasons of growing.

---

* A license to produce *GOLDIE, MAX & MILK* does not include a performance license for any third-party or copyrighted recordings. Licensees should create their own.

LISA. And then one summer, Mommy Lisa travelled to a big city for work purposes. And the city sparkled; Mommy Lisa began to sparkle; and when she returned home she was not content. So, Mommy Lisa pulled Mommy Max out of the garden, out of the home which they didn't even own, having missed the entire housing boom like losers, and they went together to the city.

And Mommy Max grew like a pumpkin, with a seed inside her. That's you.

But Mommy Lisa grew like – did you ever read that part in *Alice in Wonderland* where Alice eats the wrong thing and busts out the roof of the White Rabbit's house, and the forest creatures shame her and pelt her huge head with tools?

Mommy Lisa grew in the *wrong way*. She f-u-c-k-ed the *wrong person*. She wrecked her house.

Why would Mommy Lisa do this? Why do grownups leave their gardens and break their homes? Why can some grownups dig root vegetables and age softly and settle in, while others set fires, cause wreckage, and wander?

What is it like to be just born? What's it like to view the world through eyes that have not yet set their color? What's it like to feel air in your lungs for the first time? Does the change hurt? Is that why you cry?

> *(The desk phone beeps.* **LISA** *picks up. Baby cries again.)*

This is Lisa. *Now?* Send them up.

> *(Hangs up.)*

Do you think Mommy Lisa can become new again? But also whole, and innocent? Do you think we could do that together? Start over?

(LISA reaches into the carrier, but is terrified to pick up the baby, so she strokes her head a little instead.)

Please stop crying. Happy ending. Happy ending.

(MAX and MIKE enter. MAX goes straight for Lakshmi, picks her up, holds her close.)

MAX. My baby. My little Lakshmi. Oh my god. My baby.

MIKE. *(To LISA.)* Sorry.

LISA. Forgiven.

MIKE. Lucky guess.

LISA. We wanted to be found.

(MAX notices the bottle.)

MAX. **FORMULA?**

LISA. It's organic.

MAX. Do you have any idea what that does to her suck reflex? To my milk supply?

LISA. She loves it.

MAX. Lakshmi Rose is one hundred percent breastfed!

LISA. Don't be such a purist.

MAX. Not everyone likes a little of both, Lisa.

(Beat.)

MIKE. Um, maybe I should –

MAX. Why was she crying in the carrier? Why didn't you hold her?

LISA. I held her. But then I thought she needed to rest.

MAX. This is where she rests. Right here. Oh my god. You are right here.

LISA. Can I get you guys a drink?

MIKE. Whatcha got?

LISA. Whatever. He's stocked. Let's celebrate.

MAX. Is this the infamous desk?

LISA. I'm sorry you read that one.

MAX. Me too.

MIKE. Whoa, sis...the *desk*?

LISA. Shut up, Mike.

MIKE. When you go het, you *go*.

MAX. Shut up, Mike!

MIKE. You know what? I'll stay sober. Peace out.

MAX. Wait!

(**MIKE** *exits.*)

LISA. She pooped. I dealt.

MAX. I should have you arrested.

LISA. I took our child for a walk.

MAX. To Manhattan?

LISA. She has a carseat.

MAX. Why don't you go make a baby with Mr. Virile? Get your own hemorrhoids, and your own scar, and your own judgmental lactation consultant; then you can call yourself a mother.

LISA. Very Family Values.

MAX. Politics won't love you back.

LISA. So everything we talked about comes down to your uterus, your child? I don't want to live in those limits.

MAX. You chose this. Not me. You saw our "paths diverge in a dream."

LISA. Please don't quote out of context.

MAX. It was a lot worse IN context.

LISA. If I were a bio dad, and I had an affair while you were pregnant, I'd still be the dad.

MAX. Well, you're not.

LISA. So you plan to use heterocentrist law against me. Don't you have an obligation to the community?

MAX. Wait what.

LISA. It's 2009! Equality dawns, patch by patch, state by state! In Jersey, we're married! In Connecticut, we're married! In New York we don't have crap but change will come! We will be recognized and we will be free!

MAX. I can't believe you are initiating this conversation on this desk.

LISA. Lakshmi still has her copy reflex. Watch, I go:

> *(Sticks her tongue out.)*

And she goes:

> *(Sticks her tongue out again.)*

MAX. She's hungry.

LISA. So nurse.

MAX. In his office?

LISA. Or I can use the bottle.

> *(**MAX** nurses the baby, trying not to expose her breasts. Lakshmi cries.)*

MAX. Oh my god.

LISA. What's the matter?

MAX. She's choking on all this milk.

LISA. Does she need CPR?

MAX. No you batwing, just. Hang on.

> (**MAX** *hands Lakshmi to* **LISA**, *turns away,*
> *squeezes milk out of her breast.*)

LISA. Are you pulling the milk out of your boob?

MAX. Look elsewhere, would you?

LISA. That is intense.

MAX. Give her back.

> (**LISA** *hands the baby back.* **MAX** *gets settled*
> *nursing, again trying not to expose her*
> *breasts.*)

LISA. What happened?

MAX. I must have built up too much milk, what with her
being abducted and all.

LISA. We handled it well though, right? As a team?

MAX. You're kidding me.

LISA. Let me come clean with you, Max, in terms of the
law. I love you. I want to be with you. I want to work
through everything about me that caused me to do
what I did, and also everything about you that caused
me to do what I did.

MAX. Shut up.

LISA. You're insecure. You didn't think you could finish
your master's. I did support you.

MAX. In Portland –

LISA. In Portland you worked at the same shelter for ten
years, and talked about quitting for nine.

MAX. But I didn't quit.

LISA. Is that good?

MAX. It was good for those women.

LISA. We're in the wild west here, legally speaking. With no right to marriage we have no right to divorce. So. There is an expensive, acrimonious, court-based path in which, frankly, I'm holding all the cards. Because a liberal judge will recognize that we had a domestic partnership, from which a child resulted, or a conservative judge is going to grant some kind of rights to the father.

And then there's working things out on our own. With love.

MAX. But you found someone else.

LISA. It's over.

(**MAX** *didn't know this.*)

MAX. Tired of his desk?

LISA. He's too hairy.

MAX. Secondary sex characteristics. Shoulda thought of that.

LISA. He doesn't want more kids.

MAX. And you're just now finding this out?

LISA. He changed his mind.

MAX. So change it back. Your specialty.

LISA. I mean: he changed his mind. About me.

MAX. Oh.

LISA. Yeah.

MAX. Thus my big chance to reunite.

LISA. No, Max, I was coming to this either way, I swear!

(*Pause.* **MAX** *stops nursing.*)

MAX. Well, fuck him.

LISA. Yeah.

MAX. He's crazy.

LISA. You think?

MAX. Passing up a chance to wreck his family for a nice girl like you?

LISA. You're making fun of me.

MAX. That's right.

(**LISA** *bursts out laughing.*)

LISA. Fuck him.

MAX. Boys are gross.

LISA. They are.

MAX. You know that now. Up close.

LISA. Right.

MAX. You didn't like it?

LISA. Sure. No.

MAX. Because he's gross.

LISA. Right.

MAX. All that money. All that low hanging slung-around white guy privilege. You didn't like it.

LISA. Right.

(**LISA** *grabs* **MAX** *and tries to kiss her. They stay in some kind of embrace.*)

MAX. That Jewish girl swallowed a bottle of pills from your brother.

LISA. Oh my god.

MAX. She's at Maimonides.

LISA. Will she be okay?

MAX. They don't know. Mike went back there.

LISA. Her mother must be going insane.

MAX. Do you know what you did to me? Taking this baby?

LISA. It was a stupid move. I'm desperate for you.

MAX. Me too.

LISA. I crave our life.

MAX. Were you always like this, or did you snap?

LISA. I snapped. I'm back. Should we get over there?

MAX. We are not we.

LISA. You get over there. I'll get over there. If you want, we can share a cab.

MAX. Get your own cab.

LISA. Whatever you need.

Scene Four

*(The hospital. **SHAYNA**, clammy and disoriented, is having severe abdominal cramps, as expected. **GOLDIE** strokes her brow as **MIKE** holds a bucket to her mouth.)*

SHAYNA. OW! OW!

GOLDIE. *(Repeatedly.) Ana elna rafana la.* [Please God heal her now.]

SHAYNA. Ugh. OW. Ow.

GOLDIE. That's right. Talk, Shaynele.

      *(**SHAYNA** vomits into the bucket.)*

MIKE. *(Encouraged, not disgusted.)* Good job. Gold star.

      *(**MIKE** takes the bucket towards a bathroom.)*

GOLDIE. Oh my baby. Oh my beautiful blessing.

SHAYNA. More.

GOLDIE. More!

      *(**MIKE** doubles back with the bucket. **SHAYNA** vomits.)*

MIKE. Right on. Way to go. Upchuck all toxins.

GOLDIE. Where's the nurse?

MIKE. She'll be back. Too much sickness in this borough.

GOLDIE. Go look.

      *(**MIKE** exits with the bucket. **GOLDIE** wipes **SHAYNA**'s face, holds her, climbs into the hospital bed to get as close as she can.)*

SHAYNA. Mama.

GOLDIE. Baby.

SHAYNA. I don't wanna get married.

GOLDIE. You're better, thank God.

SHAYNA. I don't wanna go to Stern.

GOLDIE. We have time.

SHAYNA. Mama, I want to die.

GOLDIE. You made a mistake.

SHAYNA. I am a mistake.

GOLDIE. Nothing about you is a mistake. You are my precious, my first...

SHAYNA. You don't know.

GOLDIE. What couldn't I know, huh? About you?

SHAYNA. Really?

GOLDIE. I know the freckles you can't even see.

> (**SHAYNA** *drifts out.* **GOLDIE** *holds her.* **MIKE** *half-enters with the empty bucket, shifts around in the doorway, then leaves, still holding the bucket.)*

> (**GOLDIE** *sends a text message.)*

Better, thank G dash D.

> (**GOLDIE** *stares into the distance.* **MAX** *enters, holding Lakshmi.)*

MAX. Look at your baby. Your sleeping miracle.

> (*Both* **WOMEN** *watch* **SHAYNA** *through the following, rather than each other.)*

She brought me some kugel. I thought it was from you.

GOLDIE. No.

MAX. I figured that out.

GOLDIE. You want a kugel, I'm happy to make you a kugel.

MAX. I don't even know what's in kugel.

GOLDIE. It varies.

(*Pause.*)

MAX. You raised a great kid.

GOLDIE. Your opinion I don't need.

MAX. Okay.

GOLDIE. Great how?

MAX. A lot like her mom. Comfortable with the baby right away. Smart, confident, curious.

GOLDIE. I am less curious.

MAX. I'm just going to say…as a social worker. Gay teenagers are four times more likely to / attempt suicide –

GOLDIE. How dare you –

MAX. Rising to up to nine times more likely, in a rejecting family.

(**SHAYNA** *wakes.*)

SHAYNA. Hi, Max!

GOLDIE. Max is leaving. She found her baby.

SHAYNA. Someone took Lakshmi?

GOLDIE. Say bye-bye little baby.

SHAYNA. Was it Lisa?

(**GOLDIE** *spins on* **MAX.**)

GOLDIE. Now she knows *Lisa*?

SHAYNA. From Max's.

GOLDIE. I thought you're separated!

SHAYNA. It got messy.

GOLDIE. Ach, what a life.

SHAYNA. Mama, I think I might –

> *(Lakshmi cries. **MAX** puts her to the breast, not even thinking about it.)*

GOLDIE. Beautiful latch!

MAX. Thanks.

GOLDIE. So natural!

MAX. I can finish up in the hall.

SHAYNA & GOLDIE. Stay.

GOLDIE. I don't want to interrupt the session.

MAX. Lakshmi interrupted. Shayna was –

SHAYNA. No I wasn't.

GOLDIE. Shayna was curious, about the drugs. We don't have that in our community. Shayna Brucha was curious, so she experimented, with drugs. But now she's all cleaned out, thanks to your supply guy. Mike delivers all kinds of substances, huh? Boy what a useful person.

(The nursing.) Have you got the knack or have you got the knack? Here, let me show you a hold that might be more comfortable.

MAX. Shayna, why did you come to my house tonight?

SHAYNA. To see if it was as bad as everyone says.

MAX. And?

SHAYNA. You're nuts, both of you. You tell her to go; she walks in with a key. No one knows how to change a diaper. The baby suffers.

GOLDIE. I wouldn't wish such a life on a *goyishe* dog.

SHAYNA. You're lonely, and your baby's your big love. That's sick. Excuse me, but it's what I believe. It's how I was raised.

MAX. I made a mistake.

SHAYNA. You don't have a claim to your own flesh and blood.

MAX. Yes I do.

SHAYNA. Where are the laws, huh? What's written down? Some kook comes to take your baby, and you don't even know – is it her baby is it my baby is it the druggie brother's baby? What are you, writing law as you go along?

MAX. Actually, yeah.

SHAYNA. Who can live like that?

MAX. What's the alternative?

> (*Silence from* **SHAYNA**.)

I made a serious mistake. I told your daughter to do everything she could not to end up like Lisa and me.

SHAYNA. I'm not like you.

GOLDIE. See?

SHAYNA. I am so good at memorizing law, you have no idea.

GOLDIE. End of story. We all go home to a nice meal.

MAX. Shayna. Can you promise your mother you won't try again?

SHAYNA. I promise.

MAX. Can you swear to God?

> (**SHAYNA** *is silent, long enough for* **GOLDIE** *to understand she cannot swear to God. Lakshmi makes a small sound.*)

GOLDIE. *(Shaken.)* I'll take her.

MAX. She's fine.

GOLDIE. Her I can help. This one...

> (**GOLDIE** *indicates* **SHAYNA**. **MAX** *passes the baby to* **GOLDIE**, *sits by* **SHAYNA**.)

SHAYNA. Are you going to kiss me?

GOLDIE. I will drop this child.

MAX. I'm not going to do anything physical with you; I said that.

SHAYNA. I never asked.

MAX. Fine, you never asked.

> (**MIKE** *enters, hovers in the doorway.*)

What do you want from this gift which is your life?

SHAYNA. Same as everyone else. Love. God. To live on the same block as my sisters.

MAX. I don't want to live near your sisters.

SHAYNA. They're awesome.

MAX. They look up to you.

SHAYNA. They do what I say.

MAX. They could have lost you.

SHAYNA. Same difference. They're gonna pretend I'm dead anyway.

MAX. That's not true. Look at me.

> (**MAX** *holds* **SHAYNA**'*s chin and turns her face as if she were a little girl having a silly thought.*)

Your family loves you no matter what. No one's going to pretend you're dead.

(Confirms with **GOLDIE**, *no doubts.)*

MAX. Right?

GOLDIE. We don't live in your Brooklyn.

MAX. Where the fuck do you live?

GOLDIE. Lucky Lovey Rose, her mother's a beautiful accepting person in a honey jelly world. But Shayna gets me. And with me she gets –

MAX. A fence? With barbed wire?

GOLDIE. You don't judge, I don't judge.

MAX. You do judge.

GOLDIE. So, judge. Go back to your broken house and judge. Your wonderful style of a life. My daughter doesn't want a part of it.

MAX. Fine, but her methods make me worry.

GOLDIE. Shayna Brucha needs to know there are consequences.

MAX. What about you, Goldie Friedenthaler? What do you need to know that you weren't born knowing? Anything?

GOLDIE. I'm confused about plenty, thank you very much.

MAX. Tell Shayna she has a home with you forever.

GOLDIE. I have to live with my husband.

MAX. How about living with yourself? You're trying to teach me to be a mother? If you end up back in this hospital in a month, a year, with a different outcome, how are you going to live with yourself?

> *(**LISA** enters past **MIKE**, holding a showy "Get Well" floral arrangement.)*

LISA. Shayna, these are for you.

SHAYNA. Wow! No one ever gave me flowers before.

GOLDIE. She's allergic.

SHAYNA. I am not.

GOLDIE. You are now.

MIKE. I'm glad you're better, Shayna.

SHAYNA. Thanks.

MIKE. I mean, really glad.

SHAYNA. Really thanks.

MIKE. I mean, consequences. Whoa.

SHAYNA. I don't mind consequences.

MIKE. When you get to be my age, things look a little different. It all starts to count.

LISA. Mike is right. We need to make very wise choices from now on. We need to all forgive, and work together.

MIKE. Um, that's not what I –

GOLDIE. I'm sorry, but Shayna Brucha cannot accept your gift.

LISA. You must be Goldie.

GOLDIE. You have some nerve.

LISA. Thank you for everything you've done for Lakshmi Rose. Max says you're a miracle worker.

GOLDIE. Miracles happened before our era.

LISA. It's an expression.

GOLDIE. Excuse me, I only know the expression of milk. It is my sole achievement. Helping others to express milk.

LISA. I'll hold her now.

GOLDIE. Maxine?

MAX. No.

GOLDIE. No.

LISA. This is a stressful time for everybody. Maybe you don't understand –

GOLDIE. I will never understand. But you're not touching this baby.

> *(Baby cries.)*

> *(To* **MAX**.*)* She wants you.

MAX. She just ate.

GOLDIE. Let her on again.

MAX. She was on for an hour.

GOLDIE. You think it's easy being a mother?

MAX. Do you?

LISA. It could be easier, with the right support.

GOLDIE. Your baby needs you.

SHAYNA. She's gonna need you for a while.

MAX. Bring her here.

LISA. I said I could take her!

> *(***GOLDIE*** brings the baby to* **MAX**, *who nurses again, for the rest of the scene.)*

MIKE. The universe is a vast and merciful mystery. Lakshmi was missing, and now she is found. Shayna tried to kill herself, and now she is snuggling with Max.

LISA. Because she wants to fuck Max.

SHAYNA. Shut up!

MAX. Show some respect for religion.

LISA. Religion? You wanted to be a Wiccan.

MAX. In college.

LISA. You believe in nothing.

MIKE. Max believes in the soul.

LISA. Bullshit.

MAX. I've changed. I believe in the soul.

SHAYNA. You do?

GOLDIE. It's a different soul.

MAX. You live in a different Brooklyn; I believe in a different soul? No. One Brooklyn, one soul. We are all in one room, speaking one language. What do you think about that?

MIKE. Goldie prays in some funky script.

MAX. Have you never seen Hebrew?

SHAYNA. It's Yiddish.

MAX. Who cares?

SHAYNA. They're totally separate languages that happen to share an alphabet.

MAX. Whose side are you on?

SHAYNA. Yours.

GOLDIE. Shayna Brucha!

SHAYNA. I don't want to be, I don't want to be, I don't want to be...but I am.

> (**SHAYNA** *buries herself in* **MAX***, next to the baby.* **GOLDIE** *retreats.*)

MAX. It's going to be okay.

SHAYNA. How can you say that?

MAX. Maybe like your plan Z version of okay.

SHAYNA. I have nothing without my family. Nothing.

MAX. Look at me. Or don't look at me, you don't want to
be like me. Look at yourself. You have yourself.

SHAYNA. Big deal.

MAX. It is a very big deal. You have your soul.

SHAYNA. Not the way I believe it.

MAX. Okay, you have a vague non-denominational version
of your soul.

(A new offer.) You have me.

SHAYNA. I do?

MAX. If you need help.

SHAYNA. I do?

MAX. That's a promise.

SHAYNA. Do you swear before God?

MAX. I swear before Lakshmi.

SHAYNA. That works.

MAX. I will help you. Just don't hurt yourself.

SHAYNA. I won't.

>   *(Pause. **GOLDIE** watches **MAX** and **SHAYNA**.)*

LISA. I'm here for you, too, Shayna.

>   *(Tries to hand off flowers to **MIKE** so she can
>   go to **SHAYNA**.)*

Find a place for these.

MIKE. Lisa. I am. No longer. Your bitch.

LISA. *(Giggles.)* Okay...

MIKE. I am not carrying out any more of your schemes.

LISA. What schemes?

MIKE. I am not her dad. That was not our deal. And I will not further participate in any kind of case against Max, based on any idea that I am a father. Which I hope one day to be, but like, in a true and ready way.

MAX. When do you stop?

LISA. Max needs help.

MIKE. Max is supreme. Check her out. She is like the Earth. She is a natural born mama bear. Nine days with an infant, and she is mother to us all.

MAX. I am? Wow. You know, my mom...is kind of...cold?

LISA. Joan sucks.

MAX. I guess.

LISA. And she's a homophobe.

MAX. She is?

LISA. She never liked me.

GOLDIE. Imagine.

LISA. She's all over your brother's kids. Face it, Max, she rejected you; she just won't admit it because she's a Democrat. You should confront Joan. Call her on her shit. You deserve more.

MAX. I'm just trying to give better than I got.

GOLDIE. Maxine, you are overflowing.

> (**MAX** *checks her shirt – no leaks.*)

From here.

> (**GOLDIE** *hits her own heart.*)

This is your milk.

MAX. What will you do about Shayna?

GOLDIE. Shaynele and I will take a camping trip.

SHAYNA. Outside?

GOLDIE. We will sleep outside.

SHAYNA. *(Skeptical.)* With animals?

GOLDIE. We will pack a...

MAX. A tent.

GOLDIE. We will pack a tent. Soon, before it gets cold. We
   will have a wonderful trip, in all kinds of wilderness. We
   will watch the world as it is. Animals, flora, a waterfall
   even. We will learn about one another. We will become
   very close, as a mother and her firstborn should be, and
   we will take a lot of pictures.

   Because it seems that there will come a day when you
   no longer return home. And I love you like my right
   arm and both my eyes. So to live without you forever,
   will take some preparation.

SHAYNA. I'm not going anywhere, Ma.

GOLDIE.   Stay as long as you can. As long as you are
   studying, as long as you are a child, stay. But you will
   want love. And love will take you from me.

SHAYNA. It's five stops to Park Slope.

GOLDIE. I'm not counting stops.

SHAYNA. I know.

GOLDIE. Will you come on the trip?

SHAYNA. Yeah.

GOLDIE. Good.

SHAYNA. And after?

>   (**GOLDIE** *is silent.*)

   And *after*?

>   (**GOLDIE** *is silent.*)

MAX. Goldie you'd better change your mind in the woods. You'd better watch those bears.

>   (**GOLDIE** *is silent.*)

Because if not… if after all you've done for the mothers of Brooklyn, you turn away your own child, her family will be me. A single lesbian mom fighting everything your husband holds dear.

GOLDIE. I understand.

>   (*Pause.*)

LISA. Wow.

MAX. Yep.

LISA. Do you want to get back together?

MAX. I loved you a long time. Better than I thought I could ever love anybody. But you know what? I love her more. I had a hard time protecting myself, but I will protect Lakshmi Rose. And if you come for her again, legally, physically, if you come for her in any way, I will rip you in half.

LISA. So we're selling the house.

MAX. Yeah we are.

>   (*Small pause.*)

LISA. Wanna hire Mike to repaint?

MIKE. Get a professional.

LISA. You need a job.

MIKE. For everyone's information, I am applying to school.

LISA. In what?

MIKE. Pharmacology. I'd like a better grasp of the effects of my trade.

SHAYNA. Cool.

MIKE. One high of your choice for free.

(**GOLDIE** *rings the nurse button.*)

GOLDIE. Where is that nurse?

MAX. Get some rest.

SHAYNA. You too.

MAX. One of these days.

MIKE. Do you think maybe sometimes I could visit? Just to know Lakshmi?

MAX. I want her to know you.

MIKE. Awesome.

LISA. Can I come? With Mike? Ever?

MAX. We'll see.

LISA. I'll set up a college fund.

MAX. That's –

LISA. In your name. She's yours. It's obvious, even to me.

MAX. She wouldn't be here without you.

(**MAX** *checks Lakshmi, who has fallen asleep, and adjusts her off the breast.*)

LISA. Oh my god, has she been sucking on your boob this whole time?

MAX. She likes to eat.

LISA. Better you than me.

GOLDIE. Amen.

Scene Five

*(The apartment, winter. The walls are
repainted and the ceiling is fixed.* **MAX***, alone
and energized, seals up cardboard boxes for
her move. She takes a few photographs.)*

*(***SHAYNA*** enters from another room, again in
a long denim skirt.)*

SHAYNA. Wow.

MAX. Empty.

SHAYNA. Peaceful.

MAX. How's Lakshmi?

SHAYNA. Still sleeping. The movers are coming ten o'clock?
That's now.

MAX. Let her sleep. We'll do her room last.

SHAYNA. Finally you buy a crib and she has to move.

MAX. She won't even remember this place.

SHAYNA. That's why you're taking pictures?

MAX. So Lakshmi Rose knows where she started.

SHAYNA. You want I should rip a hole in the ceiling?

MAX. Smartass.

SHAYNA. Is this gonna take all day?

MAX. I don't know.

SHAYNA. I have exams.

MAX. Goldie and I planned it for Sunday so you could
help without breaking the Sabbath, so you'd better
freaking help.

SHAYNA. What have I been doing?

MAX. Lots. Thank you so much.

SHAYNA. When would you figure my indentured servitude is over and you should pay me?

MAX. When your mother decides.

SHAYNA. My mom doesn't care.

MAX. You live under her roof; you go by her rules.

SHAYNA. But it's temporary.

MAX. Life is temporary.

SHAYNA. Sounds like something she would say.

MAX. Goldie is wise, in certain areas.

SHAYNA. How come you majored in religion if you don't believe in any religion?

MAX. I am drawn to what I do not understand.

SHAYNA. Me too.

Can I have twenty bucks?

          (**MAX** *stares at* **SHAYNA.**)

Since you got Lisa to sell the house, and landed a job, and can afford to hire movers who'll probably charge an arm and a leg just to damage your valuables?

MAX. Here's fifty.

SHAYNA. You are going to be the most awesome mom!

MAX. Get your coat.

          (**SHAYNA** *exits.* **MAX** *takes a couple more pictures, maybe some video.*)

This is the house where you were conceived. Technically, two different rooms in this house. You were conceived in love, and a belief that family can be made in new ways, and the idea that two youngish women, against the odds, with no particular skills or support, might make something beautiful together. And it turned out to be true, though limited. The beautiful thing is you. The rest is over.

I wanted to give you a complete family, like a full set of china with teacups and soup liners and fish forks and siblings and grandpas, and a swingset, and a summer cabin.

We don't have any of that. But we will have a landlord, so hopefully our stove will light, and our roof will keep out the rain. And Shayna will help. And I will expand, because loving you I do expand, and one day maybe I will fill the difference between what you deserve, which is everything, and what you got. Which is me.

(*Doorbell rings.* **MAX** *calls to* **SHAYNA**.)

Movers! Ready?

(**MAX** *addresses herself.*)

Ready.

End of Play

www.ingramcontent.com/pod-product-compliance
Lightning Source LLC
Chambersburg PA
CBHW070638120726
47909CB00004B/1493